ME AND MY BIG

Look out world – there's a giant mouse on the loose!

Simon Cheshire has written stories since he was at school and is the author of *They Melted His Brain!*, *Totally Unsuitable for Children*, *Dirty Rotten Tricks* and three funny stories about schoolboy secret agent, Jeremy Brown – *Jeremy Brown of the Secret Service*, *Jeremy Brown and the Mummy's Curse* and *Jeremy Brown on Mars*. His stories, he claims, "are based entirely upon actual events. Only names, characters, plots, dialogue and descriptive content have been changed to make them more believable." Simon lives in Warwick with his wife and two children.

You can find out more about Simon Cheshire and his books by visiting his website, at http://uk.geocities.com/simoncheshireuk

Books by the same author

They Melted His Brain!

Totally Unsuitable for Children

Dirty Rotten Tricks

Jeremy Brown of the Secret Service

Jeremy Brown and the Mummy's Curse

Jeremy Brown on Mars

SIMON CHESHIRE

Me and My Big Mouse

Illustrations by Hunt Emerson

To Mum and Dad,
for everything

First published 2002 by
Walker Books Ltd, 87 Vauxhall Walk
London SE11 5HJ

2 4 6 8 10 9 7 5 3 1

This book has been typeset in Garamond

Printed and bound in Great Britain by The Guernsey Press Co. Ltd

British Library Cataloguing in Publication Data:
a catalogue record for this book
is available from the British Library.

ISBN 0-7445-5982-0

CONTENTS

CHAPTER ONE

George was always in trouble. Big, huge, dreadful trouble. He wasn't badly behaved, exactly. Things just seemed to happen to him.

Like the day he got a little white mouse. Mum was pleased. She thought that having a pet would be good for him. Dad was horrified.

"I hate mice," said Dad. "They – ACHOO! – they make me sneeze!"

Mr Squeaks (that was the mouse's name) twitched his tiny whiskers at Dad.

"Squeak, squeak," he said happily.

Dad ran away screaming.

Later that day, when George's friend Robbie came over, George was busy making a mouse house.

"It's got a games room, a PC and a big sofa," said George proudly.

"Cosy," said Robbie. "But where is Mr Squeaks?"

"I'm letting him have a run in the garden," said George.

"Is that wise?" asked Robbie nervously.

"He needs his exercise. He's going to be the world's best-looked-after mouse."

They went into the garden. At first, Mr Squeaks was nowhere to be seen. Then they spotted him scurrying from the shed. George scooped him up.

"He's all wet!"
cried George.
"You're all wet,
Mr Squeaks."
"And" – sniff,
sniff – "what's
that funny smell
coming off him?"
said Robbie.

George dried Mr Squeaks carefully, put him in his mouse house and spent the evening wondering what he'd been up to.

CHAPTER TWO

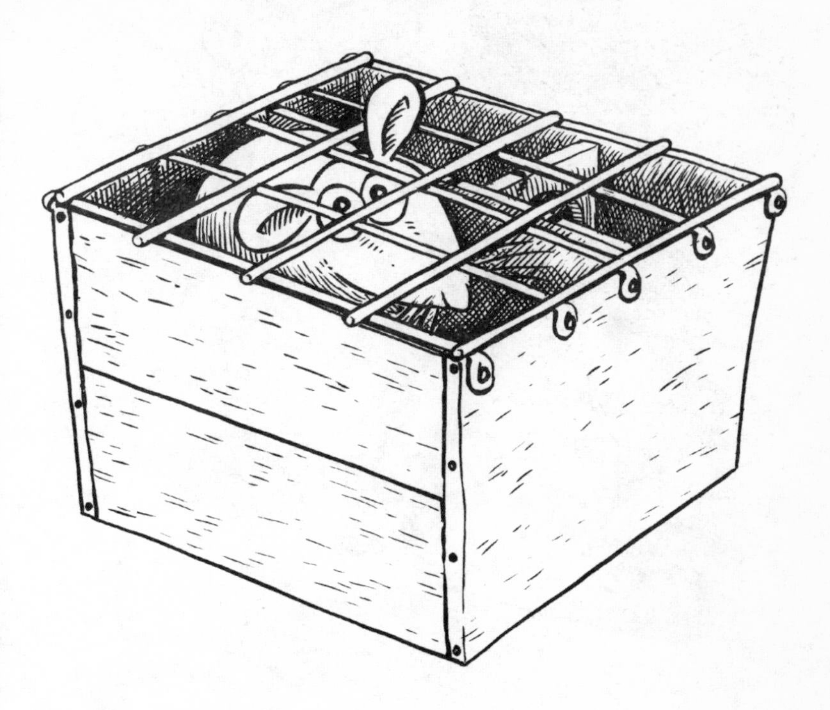

The next morning, George woke to find that he'd made the mouse house too small. Either that, or Mr Squeaks was getting bigger. He was the size of a melon.

"Squeak, squeak," said the mouse.

George was delighted. “It shows how well I’m feeding him,” he said when Robbie came over.

“But ... that’s not normal,” said Robbie nervously.

At that moment, Mum came in from the garden. "Who's used my bottle of Old Mrs Greenfingers' Growfast Ultra? I needed it for my roses!" She slapped the bottle down and stormed out.

The bottle gave off a familiar smell. The smell that Mr Squeaks had smelt of yesterday.

George looked at Robbie. Robbie looked at George.

"He fell in it!" gasped Robbie. "When he was in the shed!"

George grabbed the bottle. At the end of the instructions printed on the back was:

> Harmless to all creatures except sharks, camels and mice. It makes them grow to giant size. In the event of accidental dunking, apply Old Mrs Greenfingers' Shrinkdown Antidote.

They raced to the shed. There was no bottle of antidote. They raced back to George's room. The sides of the mouse house were bulging outwards. Mr Squeaks was wedged inside. He was now the size of a small dog. His black, apple-sized eyes blinked in alarm.

CHAPTER THREE

At first, George and Robbie felt like running away. Very fast. But running away wouldn't deal with the Mr Squeaks problem, so they went to ask Mum a perfectly innocent question instead.

"Err, Muuuum," said George, "would we happen to maybe perhaps have some Old Mrs Greenfingers' Shrinkdown Antidote lying around somewhere? Possibly?"

"Antidote?" said Mum. "No. Why?"

"Ooooo, no reason," said George. "I … umm … I think I'll pop down to SuperSave and get some."

"There's no point," said Mum. "The factory that made it went bust. It was on the news last week."

George and Robbie went white with fear.

"What do you want it for?" said Mum. "George, are you causing trouble again? George, come back here!"

George and Robbie were already halfway up the stairs. Without that antidote, Mr Squeaks would keep on growing. And growing.

"My poor mouse! We've got to keep him hidden!" gasped George.

Too late. The mouse house had burst apart. Mr Squeaks had escaped.

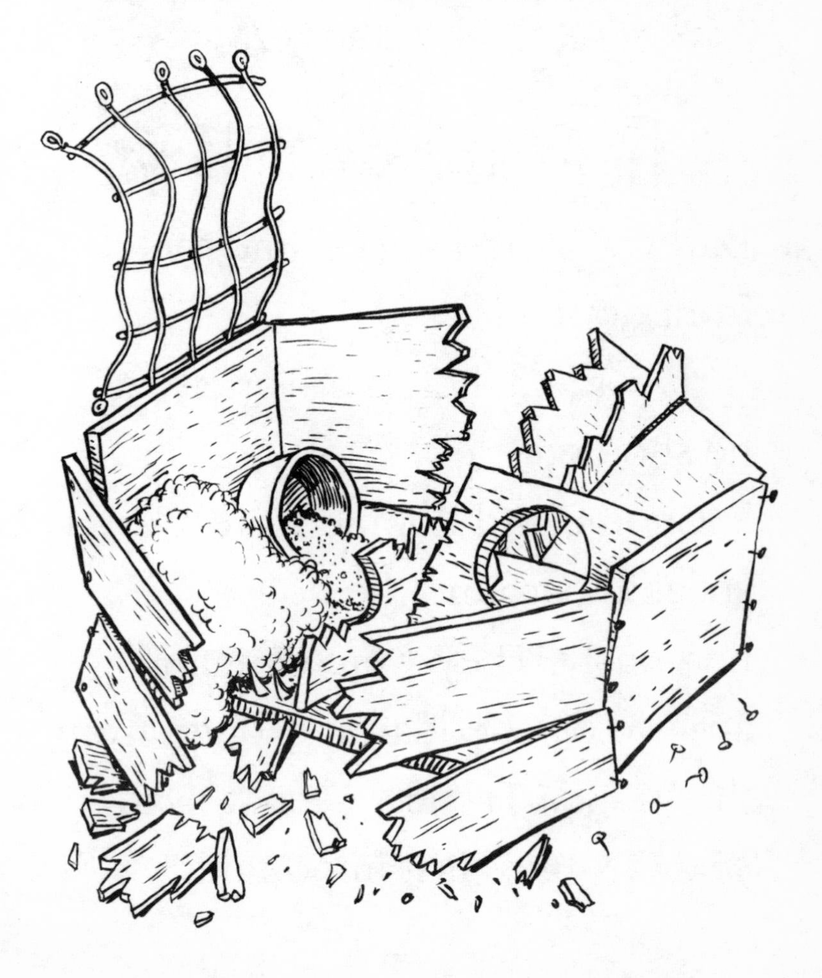

CHAPTER FOUR

Dad was searching behind the front door.

"George, where's my briefcase?" he shouted.

George and Robbie were sneaking around the house nervously. They were dangling a piece of Cheddar they'd got from the fridge. "Haven't seen it, Dad," said George. "Is it important?"

"Important?" spluttered Dad angrily. "The World Cheese Festival takes place in the park this afternoon! I am the Organizing Manager! I am having a mountain of cheese flown in specially by helicopters! That briefcase contains vital notes about— Wait a minute, what's with the Cheddar? Have you let that – ACHOO! – that ghastly mouse out?"

"No," said George quickly.

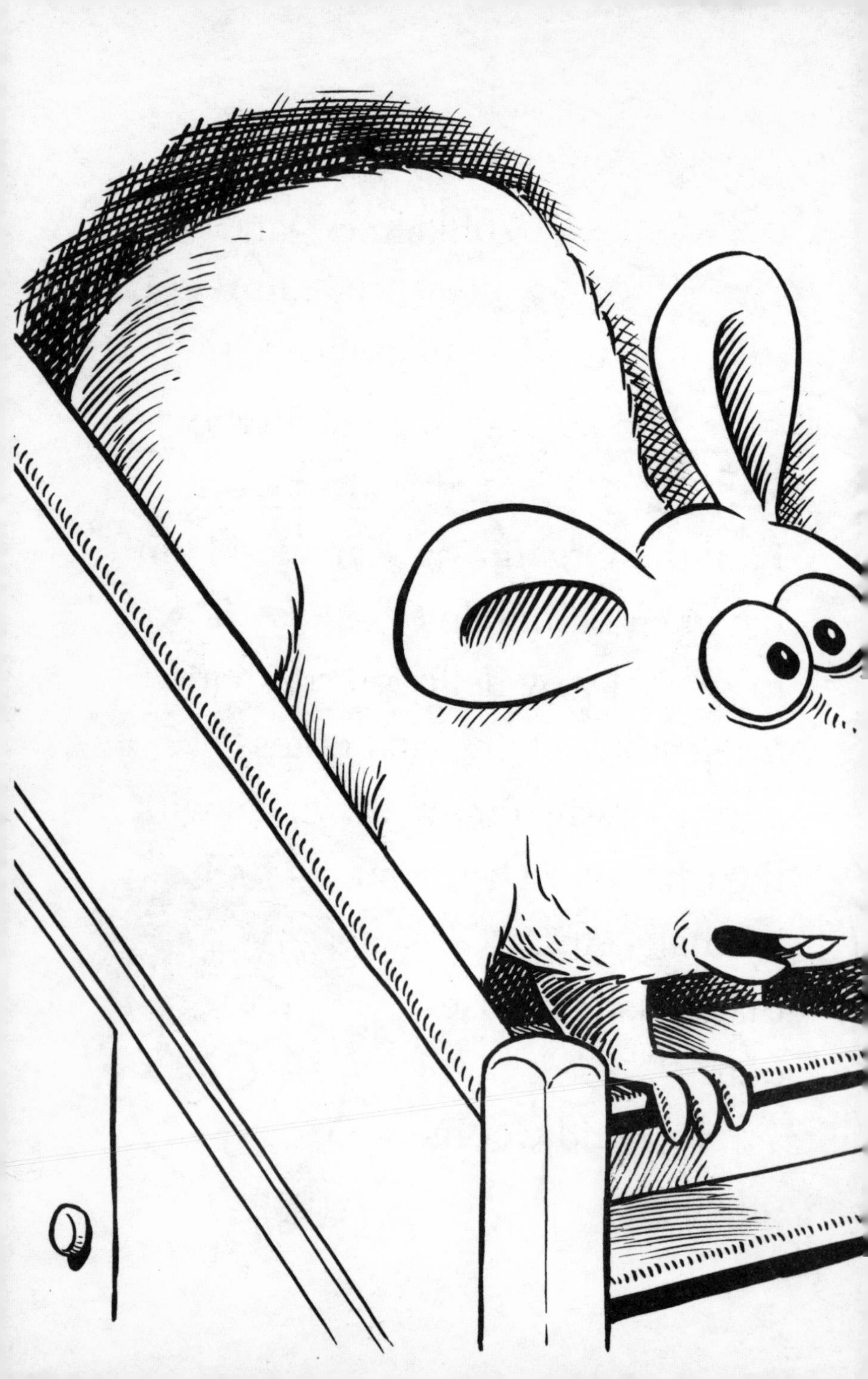

A sudden crash came from the bedrooms. Mr Squeaks squeezed down the stairs into the hall. He was now the size of a van.

Mr Squeaks dashed for freedom. He smashed through the front door and the wall around it, leaving a huge round hole.

Dad was in floods of tears. And sneezing violently.

George turned to Robbie. "Quick! Let's get into town. Someone somewhere *must* have one last bottle of that antidote. Bring the Cheddar."

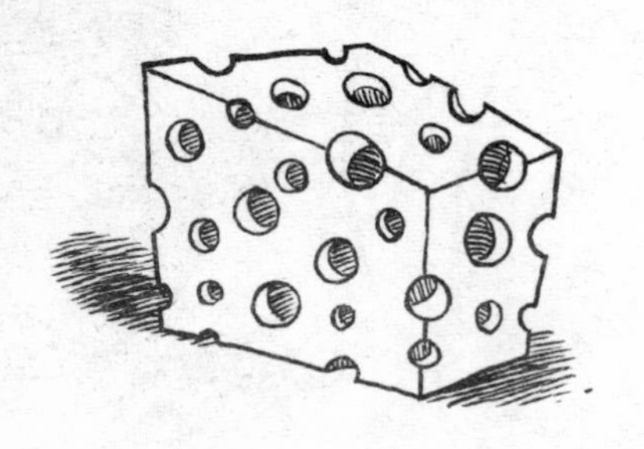

CHAPTER FIVE

Within an hour, the town centre was deserted. Police had sealed off the area following reports of a giant furry creature terrorizing the neighbourhood.

George and Robbie found their way blocked by two policemen.

"*Please* let us through," said George. "We have to search the shops for antidote."

"Sorry, your Auntie Dot will have to stay lost. There's a savage wild beast on the loose, lad," said the first policeman.

"It's his pet mouse," said Robbie. "Look, we've got a bit of Cheddar to lure him out."

"A MOUSE?" said the second policeman. "Hear that, Sarge?"

"But he *is* a mouse," said George. "Look, he's been this way! There are his droppings!"

The policemen turned. On the pavement were two mounds of mouse poo the size of wardrobes.

The policemen fainted. George and Robbie seized their chance and left.

By the time the policemen woke up, the street was deserted again. A few crumbs of George's Cheddar lay on the ground.

"Oh my stars," trembled the first policeman, pointing to the crumbs. "That vile monster has eaten those poor kiddies and made a run for it!"

"I'll call HQ!" said the second policeman, trying not to be sick. "I'll order them to bring out the giant mousetraps."

CHAPTER SIX

George and Robbie arrived at the shopping precinct.

"We'll search in here for antidote," said George.

The DIY store was dark and silent. They crept past tins of paint and rolls of lino. At last they reached the gardening section.

There, on a shelf next to the ant powder, was the very last bottle of Old Mrs Greenfingers' Shrinkdown Antidote.

George reached up for it slowly.

"Careful," hissed Robbie, covering his eyes. "That's our last hope."

George gripped the bottle and lowered it to his chest, hardly daring to breathe.

There was a loud snuffling sound. Robbie uncovered his eyes and they both turned round. Mr Squeaks was asleep right behind them, squashed into an aisle full of grass seed and houseplants. He'd snuggled down to rest in a place that smelt like his natural habitat.

"Shhh," whispered George. "All we've got to do is pop this bottle in between his teeth and our problems are over."

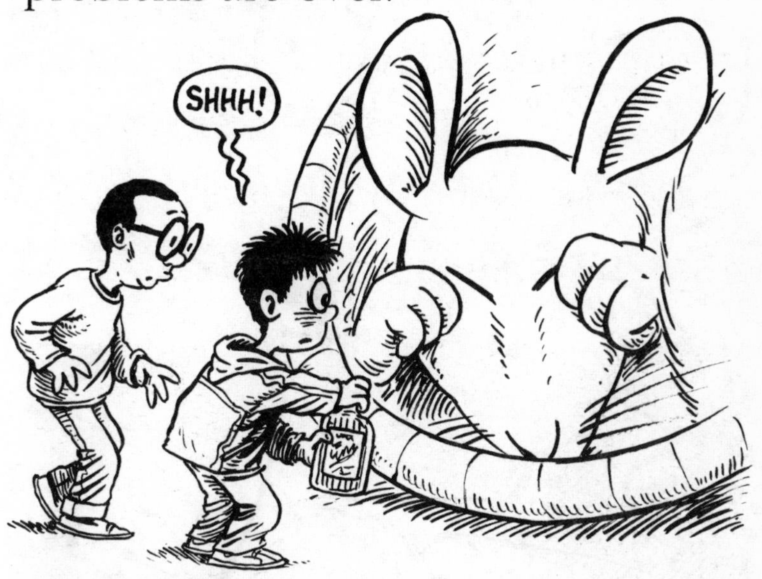

On tiptoe, they inched around his whiskers. George knelt in front of the mouse's nose and delicately unscrewed the cap off the bottle. He held it out and...

SQUEAK!

Mr Squeaks was awake! He reared up and spun around in fright. His tail whipped through the air and smacked the bottle of antidote out of George's hands.

As Mr Squeaks hurried away, the bottle twirled in mid-air. It flew in a neat curve – up, up, then down, down. George raced to catch it, but he was too late. The bottle smashed on the shop's smooth concrete floor.

CHAPTER SEVEN

"That was the only chance we had!" wailed Robbie.

"Here!" said George. "Take this!" He handed him a fluffy teddy bear from a nearby display.

"That won't cheer me up, I'm afraid," said Robbie.

"No, it's for soaking up that antidote, soppy!" said George.

Once they'd mopped up as much as they could, they headed out onto the street. Robbie looked around in a panic.

"Where do we go? Mr Squeaks could be anywhere."

"I reckon he'll make for the park," said George. "Dad ordered a mountain of cheese for the World Cheese Festival, remember? It'll be starting anytime now."

By the time they arrived at the park, the festival had already begun. Crates of cheese were being unloaded from helicopters. Marquees were full of long tables weighed down with cheese of all kinds. Cheese lovers from around the world were busily sniffing and tasting.

In the middle of it all, Dad was overseeing the whole event. He stood beneath a huge sign:

George and Robbie watched in horror as enormous mousetraps were set up around the edge of the park. The police were also expecting Mr Squeaks to turn up here.

"This is awful," said Robbie. "If Mr Squeaks doesn't go for the cheese, we'll never manage to give him the antidote."

"And if he does," said George, "he might end up in one of those traps. My poor mouse!"

CHAPTER EIGHT

"Afternoon boys," said Dad. "It's all going well. My mountain of cheese has been flown in, and everything's tip-top. George, aren't you too old for a cuddly bear?"

George clutched the antidote-soaked bear tightly. "Err, no," he said, extremely embarrassed. "I'm, err, looking after it for a friend."

Dad wasn't listening. "And no sign of that – ACHOO! – that awful, terrible mouse."

Suddenly, the ground beneath them shook. Then it shook again. With a crunching, cracking sound, the thick bushes behind the playground burst apart.

Mr Squeaks, now the size of a house, crushed three swings and a roundabout as he thundered along.

SQUEAK! SQUEAK!

"AAARRGH!" screamed Dad. "Call the police! Call the army! Call the pest control people!"

Police cars began to screech in at every entrance to the park, sirens whooping.

George and Robbie watched open-mouthed as the enormous bulk of Mr Squeaks shuffled towards the marquees.

"All we've got to do," said George, "is get this teddy into that mouse."

CHAPTER NINE

George raced to the largest marquee. No sooner was he inside than Mr Squeaks (who hadn't had a bite to eat all day) ripped it apart with his teeth. Festival guests scattered in terror, leaving a large and particularly tasty selection of cheeses untouched.

The police cars zoomed towards Mr Squeaks, their tyres digging furrows in the grass. Smelling the cheese, Mr Squeaks whirled his tail excitedly. Police cars were swatted left and right. Several of them landed in the giant mousetraps and had their engines pounded to tiny pieces.

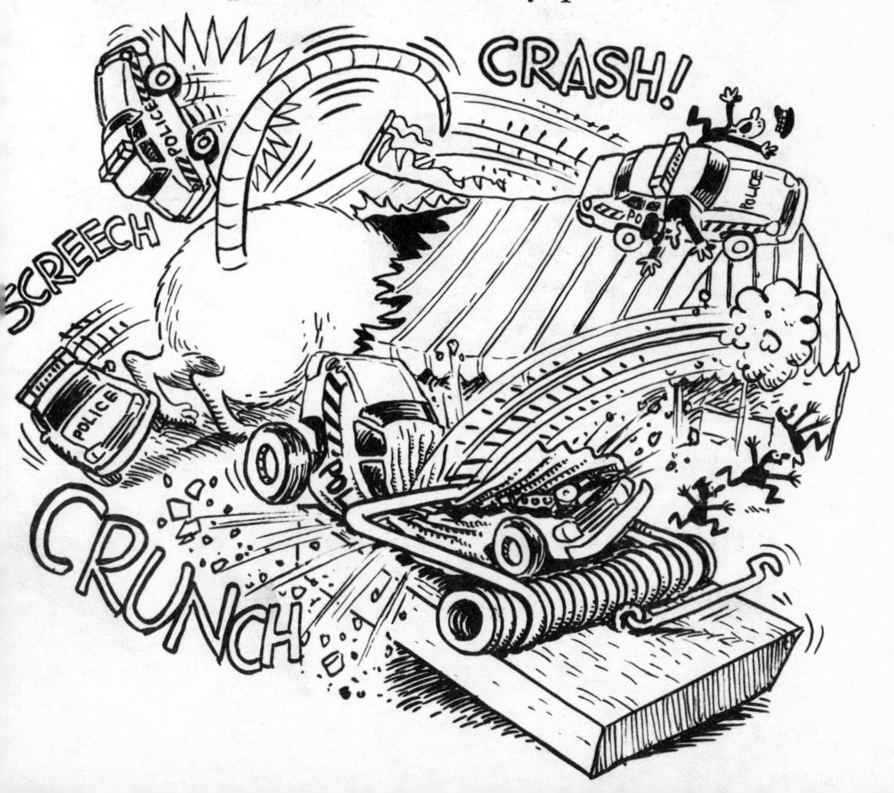

George dived for the cheese. He jammed the teddy under a ball of Edam.

Mr Squeaks' teeth closed in on the cheese. George rolled out of the way just in time. The mouse demolished the cheese, the teddy and half the table they had been sitting on.

Mr Squeaks gave a shudder and his eyes went all boggly. As George and Robbie watched, he shrank like a deflating balloon, smaller and smaller, until in a few minutes he was his right size again.

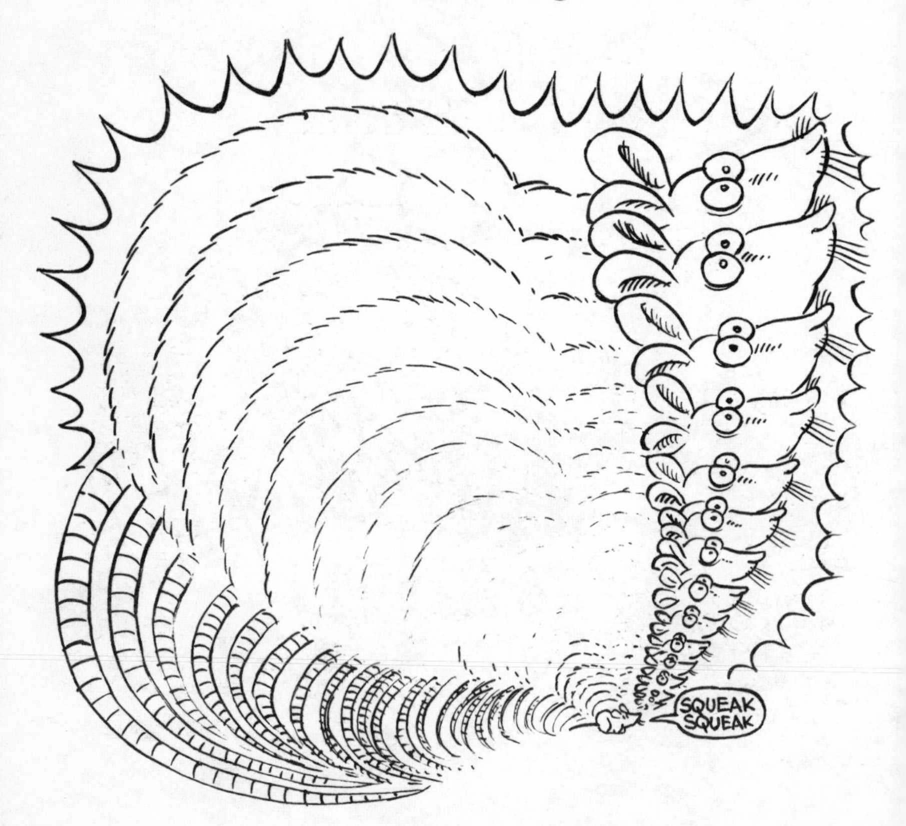

The park was still in chaos. Calmly George scooped Mr Squeaks up, cupping his hands to stop the mouse flying away. A side effect of the antidote meant that Mr Squeaks had grown tiny wings.

"I've seen it all now. I think I'll go and lie down," said Robbie.

Mr Squeaks wriggled free and took to the air. His wings fluttered quickly, making him swoop and sway as George walked along beside him. And then, together, the boy and his mouse went home.

More SPRINTERS for you to enjoy!

- *Little Stupendo Flies High* Jon Blake 0-7445-5970-7
- *Captain Abdul's Pirate School* Colin McNaughton 0-7445-5242-7
- *The Ghost in Annie's Room* Philippa Pearce 0-7445-5993-6
- *Molly and the Beanstalk* Pippa Goodhart 0-7445-5981-2
- *Taking the Cat's Way Home* Jan Mark 0-7445-8268-7
- *The Finger-eater* Dick King-Smith 0-7445-8269-5
- *Care of Henry* Anne Fine 0-7445-8270-9
- *The Haunting of Pip Parker* Anne Fine 0-7445-8294-6
- *Cup Final Kid* Martin Waddell 0-7445-8297-0
- *Lady Long-legs* Jan Mark 0-7445-8296-2
- *Ronnie and the Giant Millipede* Jenny Nimmo 0-7445-8298-9
- *Emmelina and the Monster* June Crebbin 0-7445-8904-5
- *Posh Watson* Gillian Cross 0-7445-8271-7
- *Impossible Parents* Brian Patten 0-7445-9022-1
- *Holly and the Skyboard* Ian Whybrow 0-7445-9021-3
- *Patrick's Perfect Pet* Annalena McAfee 0-7445-8911-8
- *Me and My Big Mouse* Simon Cheshire 0-7445-5982-0
- *No Tights for George!* June Crebbin 0-7445-5999-5

All at £3.99